ANGEL PARK HOOP STARS
1

NOTHING BUT NET

By Dean Hughes

Illustrated by Dennis Lyall

Bullseye Books • Alfred A. Knopf
New York

A BULLSEYE BOOK PUBLISHED BY ALFRED A. KNOPF, INC.
Text copyright © 1992 by Dean Hughes
Illustrations copyright © 1992 by Dennis Lyall
ANGEL PARK ALL-STARS characters copyright © 1989
by Alfred A. Knopf, Inc.
ANGEL PARK SOCCER STARS characters copyright © 1991
by Alfred A. Knopf, Inc.
ANGEL PARK HOOP STARS characters copyright © 1992
by Alfred A. Knopf, Inc.

Library of Congress Cataloging-in-Publication Data
Hughes, Dean.
Nothing but net / by Dean Hughes ; illustrated by Dennis Lyall.
p.   cm. — (Angel Park hoop stars ; vol. 1)
Summary: A black boy from Los Angeles has some trouble fitting in with
the twelve-and-under basketball team in his new, mostly white
neighborhood in Angel Park.
ISBN 0-679-83373-0 (pbk.) — ISBN 0-679-93373-5 (lib. bdg.)
[1. Basketball—Fiction.] 2. Friendship—Fiction. 3. Afro-Americans—
Fiction.] I. Lyall, Dennis, ill. II. Title. III. Series: Hughes, Dean.
Angel Park hoop stars ; vol. 1.
PZ7.H87312No 1992 [Fic]—dc20 92-8171

First Bullseye Books edition: November 1992

Manufactured in the United States of America

to Daniel Vosgerichian

★1★

Good News, Bad News

Kenny Sandoval dribbled to the top of the key. He fired a jump shot that banged off the back of the rim. He charged, caught the rebound, and went back up with another jumper.

The ball hung on the rim . . . rolled around . . . but fell off the side.

Kenny just didn't feel right. He was nervous.

He was warming up for tryouts for Angel Park's twelve-and-under basketball team. The league was made up of teams from several southern California towns—all little desert towns like Angel Park. The games would all be played in the Angel Park junior high gym.

More kids than usual were trying out this year. Kenny didn't know whether he would make the cut.

He was a fifth grader, and a lot of good sixth graders were trying out. Kenny was a good-sized boy, and a good athlete, but baseball was actually his best sport.

Harlan Sloan, Kenny's good friend, grabbed the ball as it dropped off the rim. He dribbled toward the corner. "Watch this," he told Kenny. "I'll show you how to do it."

He turned, dribbled once, and then let go with a long shot. The ball arched over the basket.

"Air ball!" Kenny shouted, and he laughed.

Both boys turned, however, when they saw Miles Harris walk onto the court. Miles was a sixth grader at Kenny and Harlan's school—one of the few black kids there.

He dribbled a couple of times and then leaped in the air for a long jump shot. The ball sailed to the basket like a guided missile.

Swish.

Nothing but net.

Then Miles slashed toward the hoop,

grabbed the ball, and twirled under the basket for a reverse lay-up.

The kid was *awesome*.

Miles had moved to Angel Park from Los Angeles at the beginning of the school year. He had *all* the moves. Everyone had been talking about him.

"Nice shooting," Kenny said.

Miles nodded, but he didn't say anything. He dribbled the ball outside for another shot.

Kenny could never figure the kid out. He kept to himself just about all the time. He hardly ever spoke to anyone.

"I'll bet I can stop you, Miles," Kenny said, mostly just trying to be friendly.

Miles smiled a little. He dribbled away from the basket—to the left of the lane.

Kenny moved out toward him. He spread his arms and bent forward, ready.

Miles dribbled forward. He hesitated, gave a fake to the right . . . and then *shot* past him on the left.

He drove all the way to the hoop for a left-handed lay-up.

Kenny grabbed the ball and flipped it back

to Miles. "Try again. You faked me out that time," Kenny said.

Miles was smiling a little more, but he still didn't say anything. He dribbled outside again and turned. He looked Kenny in the eyes.

Miles was not a big kid, but he was solid. He had his hair cut in a fade—short on the sides and square on top. It made him look like a lot of the college players Kenny watched on TV.

Miles bounced the ball from one hand to the other.

Kenny stayed low and ready, waiting.

And then—*bam*—Miles drove right, to the center of the key. He leaped, pivoted in the air, and popped a jump shot that ripped the net again.

"Don't you ever miss?" Kenny said.

"Sure I do," Miles said.

"Not very often," Kenny told him. "How did you get so good?"

Miles shrugged. "I've played a lot," he said. And that was all. He walked away, dribbling the ball.

Just then a whistle sounded.

Kenny looked to the side of the court and

saw big Mr. Donaldson, the coach. "Okay, players, over here! Take a seat," he yelled. "Hurry it up."

The guy sounded all business. Everyone hurried off the court and climbed into the bleachers.

Coach Donaldson gave the kids a few seconds to settle down, and then he said, "All right, now listen to me. There will be no messing around *at all.* If you can't live with that, just get up and go, right now."

No one moved.

"Second thing. We're going to break into two Angel Park teams this year. This is Mrs. Taylor over here, and she's going to coach one of the teams. That way, everyone gets to play. No one gets cut."

Kenny looked over at Harlan. He knew they were thinking the same thing: Good, but what if we get split up and have to play against each other?

Kenny was also hoping to get Mrs. Taylor as a coach. She had coached at the high school. She knew her stuff. And she wasn't always as grouchy as everyone said Donaldson was.

"Okay. It works this way," Coach Donaldson said. "If you live north of Main Street, you're on my team. We'll be called the Lakers again this year. South of Main is Mrs. Taylor's team. You'll have to pick a name."

All the kids started looking around. Kenny knew they were trying to think who lived where.

"Don't worry," Donaldson said. "The numbers come out about the same."

Kenny and Harlan lived in the same neighborhood, north of Main. That was good. But now Kenny was trying to think where all the best players lived.

"All right. Lakers move to the end of the bleachers, this way." He pointed to his right. "You others go with Mrs. Taylor, that way."

Kenny watched Miles. He took a few steps toward Mr. Donaldson's end. But he was looking back.

Everyone was doing the same thing— moving slowly and looking to see who would be on each team.

"We got Miles!" Harlan whispered. Kenny was thinking the same thing.

But then he saw Jonathan Swingle and

Eddie Boschi head the other way. They were his friends from baseball, and they were both tall.

Anthony Ruiz, another baseball player, was going that direction, too. He wasn't great, but he was big.

"Hey, they got all the tall guys," Harlan said to the coach.

"Just move down to the end," Mr. Donaldson told him. "We have a lot to do today."

But Harlan was right. The Lakers would be short. Harlan was the tallest one, and he was not a great basketball player.

Josh Briscoe and Tommy Ramirez were both sixth graders and good athletes. But they were only about Kenny's size—fairly tall for their age, but not tall enough to play center.

Miles was a fantastic player, but he wasn't all that big.

There were two girls, Jackie Willis and Stephanie Kadish. Jackie, the only other black player on the team, was good at all sports. She was quick and very smart—but not tall enough to play in the middle.

Stephanie was a little taller, but Kenny didn't think she was all that athletic.

Derek Mahana was a stout Hawaiian kid, who was a tough-as-nails football player, but . . . not very tall.

The same with Brett Sanders. He could play linebacker in football. He was maybe the second tallest, but only an inch or two taller than Kenny.

And then there was Ben Riddle, who had also played baseball with Kenny. The kid tried hard, but he was not someone who was going to help much.

The big picture just didn't look too promising.

Once all the Lakers sat down again, the coach gave them a long look. "Well, we better be quick," he said. "We sure aren't going to overpower anybody."

"Yeah, but we've got Miles," Derek said. "He can *shake* and *bake*. No one's going to stop him."

Derek slapped Miles on the back. Miles looked a little embarrassed.

The coach shot a cold, hard look at Derek. "When I want your comment, I'll ask for it.

Or if you think you have something impor-
tant to say, you raise your hand. Do you
understand that?"

"Sure."

"Yes, sir. Or yes, Coach."

"Yes, *sir.*" He suddenly sat up straight.

Some of the kids laughed.

"All right, that's enough. Maybe you don't
show respect to your teachers or to your
other coaches, but you *will* show respect to
me. What I'll give you in return is good
training, discipline, and a winning attitude.
If that's not what you want, tell me now."

Everyone was silent.

Donaldson looked the kids over. He was
a tall, square man. In his gray sweats, he
looked like a concrete wall. Even his face
was flat, with a nose that had maybe taken
an elbow shot some time.

"All right. Fine. Let me explain my rules."

And then he listed a *bunch* of them.

Missing practice meant missing the next
game. Talking back to the coach or to a referee could get you pulled from a game or
even kicked off the team. Giving less than
full effort, the same thing.

On and on he went. Kenny almost wished he had decided to play soccer with his friend Jacob Scott. This Donaldson guy was going to make life miserable.

Finally the coach handed out a practice and game schedule, and then he gave out uniforms—red and gold. He had more rules about taking care of those.

Kenny had wanted number seven, the same as he had in baseball. What he got was number twelve. But he didn't dare say anything.

When the coach was finished with all the instructions, he said, "All right. Go outside and run four laps around the outdoor track. When you get back, be ready to go hard. We're going to work harder than any team in the league."

The players stood up. Kenny was already discouraged.

Then the coach added, "We're going to *have* to work harder. The other team got most of the good players."

Thanks a lot!

Kenny stepped down from the bleachers and walked from the gym. Harlan was right next to him. "Oh, man," Harlan moaned.

"Maybe he's just coming on strong for the first day," Kenny said.

"I don't think so. He sounds *mean*."

Kenny was thinking the same thing. But he said, "Derek was right. It's lucky we got Miles. No one around here can play like him."

"Yeah. But you can't win games with one player. Besides, Miles acts like he doesn't want to have anything to do with the rest of us."

Kenny had thought that, too. In fact, he wasn't sure the Lakers had much chance of being very good.

But out he went into a cool November breeze. He had to run his four laps.

★ 2 ★

Workout

Coach Donaldson kept his word.

He had the team do a lot of drills, and most of them involved running: running forward, running backward, shuffling sideways, running while dribbling, running and passing.

And then, at the end, he had them do sprints—just to make sure no one went home with an ounce of energy left.

Kenny liked that. He liked coaches who expected a lot from a team. And he liked getting into top shape. What he didn't like was the way Coach Donaldson talked to the players—as though he didn't even like them.

The coach had the kids dribble right-handed and left-handed, drive for lay-ups, and pull up for jump shots. It didn't take long to see that some kids were a lot better than others.

Josh Briscoe was good. Jackie Willis was the best dribbler and ball handler. Tommy Ramirez was maybe second best. Derek Mahana and Brett Sanders were both fair shooters.

Poor Ben Riddle was worse at basketball than he was at baseball, but he worked hard. Kenny knew he would improve.

Stephanie Kadish was a little better than Ben, maybe, but not much.

Kenny was actually one of the better players. He was very quick, a good jumper, and a good shooter—or at least he was in his driveway at home. But now, under pressure, the shots hadn't been falling for him. And he knew why. He was letting the coach worry him too much.

Harlan was tall, but he was clumsy. Passes would slip through his hands and bang off his chest. And he was a lousy dribbler.

Still, Kenny knew that no one tried harder than Harlan. And no one had improved more at baseball. So he would do okay in time.

Of course, Miles was in a world of his own. And he did everything with pizazz.

Kenny had the feeling that two different kids were living in the same body. Miles was the silent, shy kid who kept to himself. But he was also the sizzling ball player who played like a magician.

He never shot a simple lay-up. He would hesitate and twist in the air, and then flip the ball up backward. Or he would do a three-sixty pivot on his last dribble before the shot.

Even if he missed, the other players would ooh and aah.

But not Coach Donaldson.

On Monday, the team practiced at the elementary school gym. When Miles did one of his three-sixty moves, the coach bellowed, "Harris, just put the ball in the basket. You do that showboat stuff in a game and miss because of it, and you'll be on your *butt*, warmin' the bench. Is that clear?"

Miles looked almost angry. He didn't say anything. But he nodded and said, "Yes." Then he made a "normal" shot. But a few minutes later he was cross-dribbling between his legs.

Kenny was starting to realize that Miles wasn't showing off. Moves that would be impossible for the other kids were not that tough for him. He had practiced them until they were just part of the way he played.

When practice was over, Kenny and Harlan put on their sweats. There was no locker room at the elementary school, so they had to go home to shower.

As the boys were leaving the gym, Miles came out behind them. Kenny turned around and said, "Don't let Donaldson get you down, Miles."

"I won't," Miles said, but he didn't look happy.

"At least the guy knows something about basketball," Harlan said. "Sometimes you get coaches who don't know what they're doing."

Miles nodded, as though he agreed, but then he said, "He doesn't know as much as he *thinks* he does."

"Did you have good coaches in LA?" Kenny asked.

"Sometimes. But I played a lot of playground ball, too."

"What do you mean by 'playground ball'?" Kenny asked.

A confused look came into Miles's eyes, as though he didn't understand the question.

"You mean, just getting some guys together and playing?" Harlan asked.

Miles still hesitated. Finally he said, "It's a lot more than that."

Kenny and Harlan waited. But Miles was still looking sort of baffled by the two of them.

"We had teams," Miles said. "We played every day. Outside, on the playgrounds."

"Yeah. We do that around here too. We don't have regular teams, but we—"

"No, that's not what I'm talking about. It's different. *Completely* different. Everything's different around here."

And Miles walked away.

Kenny said, "Hey, we'll see you," but Miles didn't answer.

"I don't get that guy," Harlan said to Kenny. "He acts like we said something wrong. All we did was ask a couple of questions."

"I don't think he was mad," Kenny said. "He's just had a bad day. The coach was really on him."

"Hey, Miles is always like that. I don't think the guy likes anybody."

Kenny had thought the same thing. But he had heard something new in Miles's voice this time. He just didn't know exactly what it meant.

The Lakers practiced again the next day. This time the coach started teaching the kids some offensive plays.

"All right, now listen up," he told the players. "We're small. But we have some speed. We've got to get free for lay-ups and open shots. That means we have to run a good offense."

The kids were sitting in the bleachers. Coach Donaldson was standing in front of them. With the whistle around his neck, and his short hair, he looked like one of those marine sergeants Kenny had seen in the movies.

"We're going to run a two-one-two high-post offense. We're going to set screens and free people for good shots. We're going to keep moving and wear teams down. And we're going to play defense like *maniacs*. That's the only chance we have."

No one said a word. They didn't know what he was talking about. But all the kids had learned by now that Donaldson meant what he'd said about keeping their mouths shut.

"Okay. I've picked a starting lineup for now. We'll practice today with a first and a second team. We'll run through some basic plays. I want *complete* attention so we get these down and get them right."

And then he called out the first team: "Ramirez, I'm going to try you at point guard, and Mahana, you'll play the other guard position."

Derek jumped up and threw his arms in the air. *"All right!"* he shouted.

"You sit down and be quiet, right now, before I change my mind."

Derek sat down, but he looked around at the other players with a big grin. A couple of kids laughed.

"That's enough," the coach barked. He waited a moment and then went on. "Harris and Briscoe at forwards. And Sloan, I've got you at center because you're tall. But you'll have to work your head off. You have *a lot* to learn."

Kenny hardly knew how to react.

He had sort of expected to make the first team. He thought he might be better than Derek and even Tommy. He had actually thought Jackie Willis was the best guard—and she was on the second team with Kenny.

But that was not the big shock.

Harlan was *starting*?

True, he was tall. But he was still . . . Harlan. He stumbled over his own feet.

In baseball Kenny had been a star from the first day. This was going to be something new—sitting on the bench when the game started.

He didn't want to be jealous, but it was hard not to be.

"I can't believe it," Harlan whispered.

Kenny saw the coach glance their way, so he kept his mouth shut. But he was tempted to say, "*You* can't believe it?"

"On the second team," Coach Donaldson announced, "we'll have Willis and Sandoval at guards. Kadish and Riddle at forwards. And Sanders at center. You need to learn your positions and be ready to go when you get the call."

And so the team did some hard running,

and some dribbling and passing drills. Then they went to work on the offensive plays that Coach Donaldson taught them.

He was using a lot of quick cuts off the post—plays where players ran past the center and either received passes or set screens.

Kenny didn't even know what a screen was. But he found out that it was stopping in front of a defensive player and blocking the kid from following an offensive player. The idea was to get a teammate open for a clear shot at the basket.

Everything depended on pinpoint passes and perfect timing.

Kenny worked hard to do his best—maybe too hard.

He felt awkward. And he made a couple of bad passes that got the coach upset with him.

But the pressure was on. Kenny wanted to make the starting lineup, sooner or later.

Kenny was not the only one having trouble. Everyone seemed tight. And the more Donaldson growled and shouted, the worse they played.

Except Miles. Miles did everything like a pro.

And Kenny was jealous. It was hard enough for him that Harlan had made the first team, but now a total outsider—a guy who would hardly talk to anybody—was playing circles around him.

Still, Kenny had to admit, Miles wasn't just good. He *knew* the game.

Once, Derek took a pass from Tommy, passed to Harlan, and then made his cut off the post. Harlan dropped the ball off to Derek and stood his ground.

Kenny was guarding Derek, and he did a good job of staying with him. Derek put up a shot, but it was way off line.

Kenny grabbed the rebound. When he turned around, he saw Miles walk over to Harlan.

Kenny tossed the ball out to Tommy. Then he stepped close to hear what Miles was going to say.

Miles spoke softly. "Harlan, after you pass off, always roll to the hoop. If the guard misses the shot, you're there for the rebound."

Harlan nodded, but the coach was suddenly shouting, "Hey, you guys, pay attention. Now let's start the play over."

"Coach," Kenny said.

"Yeah?"

"Miles was just saying that the center should follow the guard to the hoop—to be ready for the rebound."

"Yeah. Sure. Everyone knows that."

"Well, you didn't say anything about it to—"

"Hey, young man, don't you take that tone with me. Do you hear me?"

"I'm just saying—"

"I can't teach everything at once, Sandoval. Now you let me do the coaching." Then he shot a finger in Miles's direction. "And that goes for you, too, Harris. I don't need you talking when I'm trying to get started with some basics here."

Kenny couldn't believe it.

He glanced over at Miles. Miles rolled his eyes and shook his head just a little, but enough to get the idea across. He couldn't believe this guy either.

But for the first time, Kenny felt as though he and Miles had connected—if only for a second.

★ 3 ★

First Game

For two weeks, the Lakers practiced almost every day. Coach Donaldson kept asking the kids to come in for extra workouts.

Kenny still didn't like the guy much. But he had to admit he had never known a coach who worked any harder with his team.

Gradually the kids were doing better with the offensive plays. But with their lack of size, defense would be a problem.

So the coach had them work on playing hard-nosed man-to-man defense. And he also had them learn a zone defense that could pack the middle and put their players in position to double-team some of the tall kids they would have to guard.

In practice, the starters played defense against the second team and made them look awful. That didn't really prove much. But Kenny could tell that the starters were beginning to believe in themselves. Everyone was getting excited to start the season.

That was the good news.

The bad news was that the first game was against the other Angel Park team—the Bulls. And Kenny thought the Bulls might be the best team in the league.

But those guys hadn't been working out as much. They had a lot of good players, but maybe they wouldn't be as well prepared.

On Saturday morning, Kenny and Harlan rode their bikes to the junior high gym. "The Bulls' players don't think we're any good," Harlan told Kenny.

"How do you know?"

"Jonathan Swingle's been saying a bunch of stuff. He told me, 'Sloan, if you're in

the starting lineup, you guys must really
stink.' "

"Yeah, well, that's just talk."

But Kenny wondered. The Lakers' offense depended *a lot* on the center. And
sometimes Harlan still looked pretty bad.

But Kenny tried to keep a positive attitude.

So did the rest of the Lakers.

When they took the floor for warmups,
they cheered each other on. They told each
other it was going to be fun to beat these
taller guys.

When Harlan stepped into the center circle for the tipoff, Kenny's stomach felt like
a helium balloon.

This was it.

The Lakers had to get on these guys
early—while the Bulls still weren't expect-
ing much of a challenge.

Harlan jumped against Eddie Boschi. Eddie tipped the ball to one of the Bulls'
guards—Wes Daynes. Daynes dribbled to the
front court and then passed off to Jonathan
Swingle.

Now the defense had to show what it could do.

Josh and Derek both went after Jonathan.

And they took him by surprise. He tried to dribble, but Josh reached in and grabbed the ball away.

Miles yelled, "Here, Josh." Josh hit him with a quick pass.

And Miles was *gone*!

He shot down the court by himself. He leaped high and long and laid the ball up.

The ball dropped through the hoop. Just like that, the Lakers were up by two.

Most of the Lakers' parents were sitting behind the team, in the bleachers. They cheered and clapped. And all the Lakers on the bench jumped up and shouted.

A great start!

Across the gym, Kenny watched the Bulls' parents. They were all talking to each other—and he bet he knew what they were saying. Who *is* that kid? Where did he learn to play like that? Is he really only in sixth grade?

Kenny loved it.

For the first little while, the Bulls seemed rattled. The Lakers were *attacking*. The Bulls kept trying to dribble, and they got trapped by the double-teaming defense.

The Lakers either made steals or forced the Bulls to take hurried shots that didn't go in.

Then the Lakers ran their plays on offense. They got the ball to Miles a couple of times, and he hit the shots.

The game had only been going about four minutes when the Bulls' coach called time-out.

The Lakers were ahead 6 to 0, and they were excited. It was all Coach Donaldson could do to get them to be quiet and listen.

Kenny was hoping to get in the game soon. He wanted to get in on the fun.

But then things changed.

After the time-out, the Bulls settled down. Kenny could tell what Coach Taylor had told her players: Pass the ball. Keep it moving. Feed the tall players under the basket.

Daynes brought the ball down the court

the next time. He passed off to Jonathan.
Eddie broke toward the basket and Jonathan hit him with a quick pass.

Harlan was a little too slow on defense.
Eddie went in for an easy lay-up.

At the other end of the court, Jonathan
got on Miles like a *rash*. And another player
usually helped cover him.

Tommy kept trying to get the ball to Miles
anyway. The Bulls usually picked off the
passes.

The score was soon tied, 6 to 6.

Coach Donaldson yelled, "Tommy, never
mind Miles. Your job is to run the plays."

Tommy tried. As the point guard, he
had to choose the plays and call them. He
held up two fingers, to signal "play number
two."

Harlan took his position at the high post,
near the foul line. Tommy passed the ball
to him. Then he cut past Harlan and set a
screen for Josh. Josh brushed past Tommy.
His defender slipped by Tommy as quickly
as he could, but he was blocked out long
enough to get Josh open.

Josh broke free on the left side of the lane, and Harlan tried to hit him with a pass. But his pass was wide.

The ball bounced away. Joseph Lakey, one of the Bulls' forwards, picked it up.

Lakey tossed to ball to Daynes, who blasted away.

Daynes dribbled straight up the center of the court. A girl named Maria Tafoya—the other guard—ran with him. Tommy stayed with Daynes, but it was a two-on-one break.

Miles also ran hard. With his speed, he made up the ground fast. But Daynes hit Maria with a good pass, and she broke toward the hoop.

Miles skied through the air and slammed the ball out of bounds.

It was an amazing play. The whole crowd gasped when they saw how high Miles had gone.

But Miles wasn't finished. The Lakers got good pressure on all the players as Boschi tried to throw the inbounds pass.

When Boschi tried to lob the ball to

Daynes, Miles dashed in front of him and picked the ball off.

He was off and running, a clean break to the other end of the court. And then he gave the lay-up some dazzle. He was all alone, so he slowed, twisted in the air, and flipped the ball up over his shoulder, with his left hand.

He put some spin on the ball, and it came off the glass just right. It split the net.

The crowd went crazy. Even the Bulls' fans gave Miles a hand.

But Coach Donaldson stood up and looked at his bench. "Sanders, go in the game for that show-off!" he shouted.

And just like that, Miles was out of the game.

When Miles got to the bench, the coach was waiting for him. "Don't *ever* do that again, Harris," he grumbled.

"Hey, I hit the shot. You said if I—"

"And don't *argue* with me either!"

Miles walked as far from the coach as he could get, and he dropped onto the bench.

Kenny was worried.

The Lakers' best player was on the bench.
That was bad enough. But he could also see
that Coach Donaldson was going to keep
riding Miles until he changed. How could
the team ever get it together with that going
on?

For the next few minutes, things went
badly.

The Lakers tried to make cuts past Harlan. And they tried to set their screens. But
the bigger Bulls hovered over them and cut
off the passes.

Tommy tried to direct the plays, but
Daynes was guarding him tight. He strug-
gled to keep hold of the ball.

Josh did get loose for a jump shot that
dropped. And Derek let fly with a bomb that
bounced off the front of the iron and off
the glass. But somehow it finally fell into
the net.

At the other end of the court, the Bulls
were pumping up shots that usually missed.

But it didn't matter.

Lakey and Boschi were waiting for every
rebound. If the second shot didn't go in,

the third or fourth did. The shorter Lakers just couldn't compete under the basket.

By the time Coach Donaldson called a time-out, Kenny was starting to think the whole season might be a disaster.

The score was 18 to 10 now.

At least the coach was putting Miles back in. "Now you play basketball and quit showing off," he told Miles.

Miles nodded. But he looked angry.

Coach Donaldson also told Jackie and Kenny to replace the guards. They checked in at the scorer's table. When they came back, the coach talked to the kids about what they had to do.

"You can get those rebounds if you block out," he told them. "Harlan, Josh, Miles— you gotta fight for the ball."

Then he looked at Jackie and Kenny. "You guards need to take what the defense is giving you. They're sticking two kids on Harris. That means someone is open."

Kenny's heart was pumping. He really wanted to do well. He glanced up at the bleachers and saw his parents. His mom waved and yelled, "Okay, Kenny, get tough!"

His dad nodded to him, as if to say, "I know you can do it."

Derek yelled, "Hey, Kenny, you got some big shoes to fill. You gotta play like the great Derek Mahana."

But Kenny didn't laugh. He was concentrating. He knew he had to go hard.

When play started again, he tossed the ball to Jackie, and she brought the ball into the front court.

Then she held up two fingers for play number two.

Kenny waited for her to pass off to Harlan. Then he cut off the center. He got the pass from Harlan but was well covered. He flipped the ball out to Josh.

Josh was open, and he took the shot.

And missed.

But Miles jumped high to grab the offensive rebound. He landed, faked, and got Eddie to jump. Then he went up himself.

Eddie came down with his chest right on Miles's back, but Miles still got the shot away. The whistle sounded just as the ball dropped through the basket.

"Two and one!" the ref yelled. "Basket counts. Shooter gets one foul shot."

So Miles stepped to the line and dropped in his foul shot.

The lead was cut to five. Miles made all the difference.

At the other end of the floor Kenny went hard. He stayed tight on the player who came into his part of the zone.

When Daynes tried to force a pass to Jonathan, Kenny stepped in and stole the ball. He flipped it out to Jackie as she blasted toward the other basket.

Jackie drove the length of the floor with Daynes running step for step with her. Kenny chased after them.

Daynes got ahead of Jackie and kept her from going straight to the hoop. So she backed off and flipped the ball to Kenny.

Kenny drove for the basket as Daynes charged toward him.

Still, Kenny should have scored. He had a step on Daynes, and he only needed to lay the ball up and in. But he was nervous, and he slammed the ball too hard off the glass.

It fell off the rim and Daynes leaped for it.

And then, there was Miles, flying high. He reached above Daynes and tipped the ball back up and over the rim.

Two points.

The score was 18 to 15.

The Lakers weren't out of this game yet!

★ 4 ★

Chewed Up and Spit Out

Kenny and Jackie stayed in the game for the rest of the half. When halftime came, the Bulls were still ahead, 23 to 19.

The game looked as if it was going to be a battle all the way.

But when the Lakers reached the locker room, Coach Donaldson started shouting. "I swear, you kids forgot everything I've taught you!"

That was only the beginning.

He chewed on everyone. He especially hit Miles hard. "Harris, you're freelancing too much out there!"

Kenny could hardly believe his ears. Miles had scored more than half the Lakers' points.

But Kenny got his turn, too.

"Sandoval, what were you thinking about? You threw up shots you had no business taking. And watch your passes. We can't afford to *give* them the ball."

Kenny knew he had messed up. But he had also made some good passes. And he had knocked in a nice shot from outside. The coach didn't seem to remember any of that.

Maybe Coach Donaldson was trying to fire the players up. But it didn't work. Kenny could *see* the players losing heart.

Kenny was actually relieved that the starters were going back in now. He was scared he would do something wrong and get chewed out all the more.

When the second half got going, no one played with as much fire—not even Miles.

He tried to fit in with the offense. He could have made quick moves on his own, and gotten free for shots. Instead, he ran the patterns the coach had taught them. But he looked out of sync.

Josh was getting open at times. So was Harlan. But they missed some early shots, and the Bulls made a run.

Before long the score was 31 to 21. And the Bulls were *hot.*

Coach Donaldson pulled Josh and Harlan from the game and put in Ben and Stephanie.

When the two starters got to the bench, Coach Donaldson said, "You guys aren't playing like you even *want* to win."

Harlan whispered to Kenny, "I'm doing my *best.* I don't know what he wants from me."

Midway through the second half, the score was 43 to 27. The Lakers looked confused. Poor Ben and Stephanie just couldn't handle the bigger players—at either end of the floor.

Coach Donaldson finally called time-out. He put Josh and Harlan back in. "Do you want to play now?" he demanded. "Are you going to fight for the rebounds?"

They both nodded, but they looked scared.

The coach told Kenny and Jackie to check in, too. Kenny took a deep breath. He made up his mind not to worry about the coach and just go hard.

Jackie had more confidence than Tommy.

Kenny knew that's what the team needed right now. The Bulls were starting to get mouthy, and Kenny knew that the Lakers were trying almost *too* hard. Someone needed to calm things down.

The first time down the floor, Jackie dribbled the ball to the top of the key. Josh charged forward and set a screen on the center—a guy named Griffen, who had come off the bench.

Jackie was supposed to pass the ball to Harlan as he broke away. But Lakey picked up Harlan.

Jackie faked to Harlan but held the ball. Then she spotted Miles cutting toward the basket. She looped a pass, and he went high for it.

He caught the ball and shot—without coming down.

The ball *swished,* and the Lakers' fans roared.

Suddenly the spark was back. On defense, the Bulls missed a shot. Josh fought for the rebound. He got the ball to Jackie, and she hit Kenny with a lead pass.

Kenny took off for the other basket. He

drove hard, but Daynes darted back and cut him off before he could go directly to the hoop.

But Miles was there.

Kenny hit him with a bounce pass. Daynes leaped high to block the shot. But Miles twisted around him, and took the shot with his left hand.

The ball dropped in, and every player on the Lakers' bench jumped straight in the air.

Kenny watched the coach. He couldn't say anything about that shot. Miles had done what he had to do to get the ball in the hole.

But Miles was having fun now.

He stayed back for the inbounds pass. He put the press on Daynes and hassled him until he forced a pass. Jackie stepped in and stole the ball. She drove straight to the hoop and laid the ball up . . . *and in!*

Suddenly the score was 43 to 33, and the Lakers had a chance.

The Lakers were all yelling to each other to play tough defense. The kids on the bench was still standing up.

Kenny could feel the excitement. He stayed tough on Jason Stafford, who had come into the game as a guard. Jackie was bothering Daynes every inch of the way down the floor.

Once the Bulls crossed the ten-second line, the Lakers set up their zone. Everyone covered close.

The Bulls had a lot of subs in the lineup right now. And they were losing their cool.

Daynes stopped his dribble and then had trouble finding anyone to pass to. Finally he made a frantic toss to the forward on the left side. He "telegraphed" the pass, however, and Josh broke in front and stole the ball.

Josh passed off to Jackie, and she brought the ball up the floor. Before the defense could get set, Jackie hit Miles on the right side.

Two defenders crowded Miles, and then the center charged toward him, too. He seemed trapped, but he flipped the ball behind his back and hit Kenny with a perfect pass.

Kenny drove to the hoop.

All alone!

But as he jumped for the lay-up, he lost

control of the ball. It banged off the back-board.

The Bulls' center outleaped Josh for the rebound.

The center spun around and saw Daynes streaking to the other end of the floor. He threw a long pass, and Daynes went in for the easy basket.

Kenny had had his chance, and he had blown it!

He could have gotten the lead down to eight and kept the momentum going. Now the Bulls had them by twelve.

Coach Donaldson called time-out.

He didn't chew Kenny out, but he pulled him from the game—and Jackie too. Then he told Miles, "I want you to pass the ball the way I taught you. I don't go for that behind-the-back stuff."

And that was the end.

Tommy went back in the game and kept trying to work the offense. But the Bulls put their first team back on the floor. And they got tough.

Josh did make a couple of baskets. But Harlan missed two easy shots, close to the hoop. And Derek seemed to forget the plays and just run around.

When it was all over, the Bulls had won, 56 to 39.

That was bad enough.

But the Bulls rubbed it in *plenty*.

"It's sure good you guys had a lot of extra practices," Jonathan told them. "Just think how bad you *could* have played."

Derek told Jonathan to shut his mouth.

But the other Lakers walked away. They expected stuff like that from the Bulls. They knew all these guys from school, and knew how mouthy they could be.

Coach Donaldson was the one who hit the hardest.

"I was *ashamed* of you kids out there today," he told them.

He listed off their mistakes, and then he zeroed in on Miles. "This is not *street basketball*!" he told him. "You've got to learn to fit in to our offense. No more showing off!"

Miles didn't say a word. But he took a shower and changed quickly. Everyone else was doing the same thing.

Kenny felt rotten. He couldn't forget that he had messed up just when the team was trying to make a comeback.

No one mentioned it, of course. Kenny knew they must be thinking it, though. Or maybe they felt just as rotten about their own mistakes.

"I don't have to put up with that man," Miles said. "I'm quitting." He slammed his uniform in his duffle bag. Then he grabbed his jacket and headed out the door.

Kenny knew the whole team could go to pieces if someone didn't do something. He jumped up. "Hey, Miles, wait," he yelled. But Miles was walking out the door.

Kenny caught up with him outside. "Miles," he said, "don't let the coach drive you away. He knows you're the best player we've got. We all know that. We need you."

Miles kept walking.

Kenny glanced back and saw Harlan come out the door. He motioned for him to hurry, and then he ran after Miles. "Wait a minute, Miles."

Miles spun around. "Didn't you hear the coach? He doesn't want me. I'm a *street* player. What he really means is a *black* player. *That's* what he doesn't like."

"I don't think so, Miles. He just thinks we should—"

"I'll *tell* you what he thinks," Miles said. "He thinks I'm some dumb black kid from a bad neighborhood. But you know what? I could teach *him* a few things about basketball."

Miles was off and walking again.

"Maybe he just thinks he has to chew on us to get us to play our best," Kenny said.

Kenny and Harlan hurried to keep up.

"Listen," Miles said. "In my neighborhood, I played with guys who knew *every move* I was going to make. We played together since we were little kids. We were . . . oh, never mind. You wouldn't understand."

"We'll get better," Kenny said. "A few times today, we started to do okay. We'll get more of a feel for things when we've played together more."

"I'll never get a feel for anything around *here*."

"Why not? We can—"

Miles stopped again. He took a long, hard look at Kenny. "Kenny, you just don't know what it's like to be black in a white town like this."

"Hey, am I white?"

"Basically, yeah."

"I'm Latino. What are you talking about?"

"That's not the same, and you know it. I'm not from here, like you are. Nobody likes my style—especially not the coach. He can't stand me."

"The coach is on *everybody*," Harlan said.

"Yeah, but it's me that he hates. And I know why." Miles took a long breath. And then, more quietly, he said, "My dad brought me out here to give me *opportunities*. That's what he tells me, anyway. But every time I start to feel okay, I find out I don't fit."

"You will. It just takes a little while to—"

"You don't get the point, do you? I play hard, and all I get is, 'Don't show off. Play like the white boys do.' Well, I can't do that. I don't know how. And I don't *want* to know how."

"Okay. But don't quit the team. We'll be nothing without you."

Miles shrugged, and then walked away.

And Kenny watched him go. He didn't know what to say.

★ 5 ★

Troubles

Kenny was relieved when Miles showed up at practice on Monday. He decided he would try to be a better friend to Miles. He hadn't been sure he liked the guy at first, but now he thought he understood him a little better.

Quite a few kids in Angel Park were Mexican-American. Very few were black. That was hard enough, but Miles had moved from a mostly black neighborhood. No wonder everything seemed strange to him.

Coach Donaldson seemed to know that he had come down a little too hard on the team after the Bulls' game. He wasn't quite so grouchy, and he hardly said anything to Miles.

At the Thursday practice, however, he saw

Miles dribbling behind his back, and he told him to lay off. Kenny was relieved again when Miles didn't walk off the court.

Kenny and Harlan rode their bikes home together. Kenny told Harlan, "I don't get what the coach is trying to do. When you've got a guy as good as Miles, you can't tell him to just 'fit in.' "

"I know. But Miles does show off."

"Yeah. In a way. But maybe that's just how it looks to us. I think that's just how he plays the game. If the coach takes that away from him, Miles won't be as good."

Harlan was hunched forward on his bike. He had a stocking cap pulled over his ears. Winter wasn't very bad in the desert country, but the air was cool tonight.

"I'll tell you what worries me, though," Harlan said. "Everyone's always knocking the coach. And I don't see how we're going to be a good team if we all keep doing that."

Kenny knew that. But he remembered Coach Wilkens in baseball. The man never got angry, yet he got plenty out of his players. "Harlan, if he knows his basketball so well, how come he doesn't start Jackie instead of Tommy?"

"I don't know. I've been wondering about that, too."

Kenny *knew* she was the best ball handler on the team, and yet she was on the second team. It didn't make any sense.

"Maybe he sees some stuff that we don't notice."

"Yeah. Maybe."

But Kenny didn't say what he was thinking.

Was Miles right? Was the coach prejudiced? Against blacks? And maybe against girls, too?

That just wasn't right.

Kenny knew something about prejudice. He had experienced some in his own life. Sometimes teachers made him feel as if they didn't expect him to be as smart as white kids. But he didn't want to put up with that kind of stuff on the basketball team. He loved sports too much to see that happen.

On Saturday morning, the Lakers played the Blue Springs Warriors. Dave Weight, the star of the Blue Springs baseball team, was even better at basketball. And Hausberg, the big pitcher, would be a strong rebounder.

Cooper, Sanchez, and Dodero—all base-ball players—were also on the team. And they all looked *tough* during warmups.

But early in the game, the Lakers' start-ers worked their plays. Blue Springs wasn't very disciplined. The Lakers were able to break players loose.

The shots were falling, too.

Angel Park got off to a 10 to 3 start.

Kenny felt better. Maybe the coach's of-fense was going to pay off after all.

But Blue Springs called time-out.

"All right, Harris," Coach Donaldson told Miles, "that's what I want to see. You're staying with our plays. Just keep doing that, and we'll beat these guys."

But the Warriors' tubby little coach was talking hard on the other side of the court. When the Warriors came back on the floor, they seemed to have a better idea what to do.

Blue Springs switched to a zone defense. Weight and Hausberg clogged up the middle. It was tough for the Lakers' guards to make their cuts off the center.

The Lakers weren't getting such open shots now. When they missed, Hausberg would muscle Harlan away from the basket and grab the rebounds.

Before long, the Warriors had closed the gap to 13 to 11. Then, when Coach Donaldson put in some subs—Brett and Ben—Blue Springs got their offense rolling a little better.

By halftime the Warriors were ahead 23 to 16.

Kenny and Jackie had only gotten in the game for about two minutes, and Kenny hadn't played well. He was still too tight.

But that was not the worst.

Miles had almost disappeared. He was one gear in a machine. But the flash and action were gone from his game. He wasn't making moves to get open.

At halftime the coach didn't yell. Maybe he was too disgusted. "What in the world are you *doing* out there?" he asked the players. "When they go to the zone, you have to make quick passes. You kids are just standing around."

Kenny thought he knew what the coach really meant: "You kids aren't any good."

That's what everyone else seemed to be hearing, too. Miles was staring straight at the floor.

The team went back out on the court and played worse.

The Warriors were putting pressure on Tommy as he dribbled the ball down the floor. Close to the basket, Hausberg and Weight were all over Harlan and Josh.

And Cooper was on Miles like a shadow. One guy could guard him when he wasn't really using his moves.

By the middle of the second half the score was 35 to 20.

The Warriors put in most of their second-team players. But even that didn't seem to make a lot of difference.

Coach Donaldson finally put Jackie in the game but left Kenny on the bench.

Kenny saw Miles walk over and say something to Jackie. The first time she got the ball, she burst past her defender and then tossed the ball to Miles. He had cut toward the lane.

Miles grabbed the pass and then broke to the hoop. When Hausberg met him, he pulled up for a short jumper that went in.

It wasn't a set play. Miles had just used his quickness, one-on-one against Cooper, and he had made something happen.

Jackie had seen the opportunity and *taken*

it. But she had been looking for Miles. Kenny knew they had talked about it.

The Lakers' parents gave Miles a big hand. Kenny heard someone yell, "That's it, Miles. Go after him."

Kenny looked back and saw Miles's parents. Mr. Harris looked like a ball player—tall and strong. He was clapping his hands and still yelling. So was Miles's mom.

The kids on the bench picked it up. "Come on, Miles," Stephanie yelled. "You can chew that guy up."

And Miles seemed to make up his mind to do just that.

He made quick moves to get free. And Jackie got the ball to him. He sank two jumpers from the side of the lane. Then he faked a shot and drove to the hoop. Hausberg cut him off, but Miles shoveled the ball to Harlan.

Harlan made the easy shot under the basket.

Just like that, the score was 35 to 28.

The Blue Springs coach jumped up and called time-out. He put his first-team players back in the game.

Coach Donaldson actually seemed sort of hopeful. Kenny heard him say, "Okay, good passes, Jackie. But don't start feeding Harris all the time. Move the ball around."

The players on the bench whooped it up as the Lakers went back on the floor.

The crowd got into the excitement, too, and they started making some noise. "Let's *do it!*" Miles's mom yelled.

And it suddenly seemed they could.

The Lakers got back on defense and hustled. Weight shot a jumper from the corner, but Josh had a hand in his face. The ball rimmed around and came out.

Josh went hard to the board and came down with the rebound.

"That's it, Josh!" Coach Donaldson yelled. "Let's go."

Josh passed the ball out to Jackie. She took the ball up the field quickly. Then she passed off to Derek, who tried to feed Miles.

Miles was double-teamed now. Dodero knocked the ball away.

But Jackie shot over and picked up the loose ball and dribbled back to the head of the key.

"Work the offense," Coach Donaldson yelled.

Jackie held up a fist to signal a play.

She passed to Harlan on the high post. He faked a pass to Derek and then fed the ball to Josh. Josh went up for a jump shot that bounded on the rim and then rolled off.

But Miles charged hard.

He leaped high and grabbed the rebound away from Hausberg. He dribbled once and then faked in the air. Hausberg leaped before Miles went up for the shot.

Hausberg came down with both arms across Miles's shoulders. But somehow Miles managed to flip the ball in the air anyway. The ball bounced off the glass and rolled on the rim.

And dropped into the basket!

It was an impossible shot. Only Miles's feel for the ball could have made it happen.

He dropped a foul shot in, and the score was 35 to 31.

Kenny looked at the clock. Less than two minutes to go. The Lakers needed some big plays. And they couldn't let Blue Springs score again.

The Blue Springs coach was yelling to slow down, to work for the good shot.

Dodero brought the ball down and passed

into the middle to Hausberg. Miles broke from his man and went for the steal. He knocked the ball away, but the whistle sounded.

Foul on Miles.

"That's a smart play," Kenny told Brett, who was sitting next to him. "Hausberg has no touch. He'll miss the foul shot."

And miss he did.

Hausberg shot up a clunker that banged off the rim. Harlan grabbed the rebound and the Lakers were back in business.

"Run the offense," Coach Donaldson was shouting.

Jackie took the ball across the ten-second line. She held up one finger. She dribbled to the top of the key and seemed ready to pass to Derek.

But just then Miles dashed toward the hoop. Jackie arched a high pass to Miles, who was near the base line.

The pass was a little long. Miles reached and caught the ball anyway, and he managed to come down in bounds. He was off balance, but he went up for a jump shot.

The ball went in . . . and popped back out.

Weight grabbed the rebound.

The Lakers fell back and Blue Springs took its time coming up the floor.

This time Dodero got the ball to Weight, and Josh fouled him. But Weight was a good foul shooter.

Coach Donaldson called time-out. He sent Tommy back in the game. "Jackie, what were you *thinking*?" Coach Donaldson yelled. "I told you to run the offense."

"Miles was open, Coach," she said. "He had a good shot. It almost went in."

"You were looking for Miles all the way, Willis. You didn't even try to run the play."

Kenny heard the words, but mostly he heard the anger. He knew everyone else did, too.

He also knew the game was over.

Weight made his foul shots, but it didn't matter.

The Lakers didn't score again.

They went hard for the ball on defense. But the whistle kept blowing. And the Warriors were making their foul shots now.

The final score was 42 to 31.

The Lakers had lost again.

★ 6 ★

Victory

On Sunday afternoon, Kenny had a chat with his dad. He told him that he thought maybe Coach Donaldson was prejudiced against black people.

Mr. Sandoval listened and didn't say much. Kenny knew what his Dad always said: Players should listen to their coaches and support them. But this time he said something surprising.

"Kenny, I've faced plenty of prejudice in my life. And sometimes I've just taken it. But there are times when you have to stand up for yourself—or for others. The only thing is, you have no right to accuse anyone unless you have all the facts."

"So what should I do?" Kenny asked.

"I don't know. You'll have to decide that one for yourself. But for now, I'd say Miles needs a good friend in this town. I talked to his dad at the game. He says that Miles is having a hard time."

"Yeah, he is."

"You know, his dad moved here so he could give Miles and his sister a better life. But it won't work if Miles can't find any decent friends."

Kenny thought a lot about that. He wasn't sure that Miles *wanted* to be friends. He also didn't think he could do anything about Coach Donaldson's attitude.

He wished there were some way to make things right—and fair. He couldn't see any way to do that, though.

But he kept thinking about it all weekend.

Monday afternoon, the Lakers held practice. Coach Donaldson had the kids sit down in the bleachers first.

Then he started in on them.

"Maybe you kids don't mind losing, but I do. How can I get you to understand? We don't have size—so we have to *outthink* teams.

And that means *discipline*. Good passes. Open shots."

Kenny had some things he wanted to say to the coach about that. But he didn't dare.

"We had a chance there at the end of the game," the coach was now saying. "And then Jackie thinks she can lob a pass all the way to the base line."

Coach Donaldson was pacing back and forth in his gray sweats, his hands on his hips. He stopped in front of Jackie and looked at her. "It was a dangerous pass. And it wasn't the play you had called."

Kenny really wanted to raise his hand. He just couldn't do it.

"I guess everyone thinks I'm a hard-nosed guy. But I know what it takes to win. If anyone here doesn't like what I'm doing, just say so. Otherwise—"

Kenny's hand was suddenly in the air.

At the same time, his breath had caught in his chest. He wasn't sure he would actually dare say anything.

"Yeah? Sandoval. What is it?"

"Uh . . . I've been thinking about the offense."

"Yeah. What about it?"

Kenny took another breath. "We have a great player on our team. But I don't think our plays use him enough."

Coach Donaldson laughed and shook his head. "Sandoval, you can't build a team around one player."

"I'm not saying that. Miles shouldn't have the ball all the time—but it seems like he ought to get it more than he does."

"And let him play all that fancy one-on-one stuff? Is that what you want, Sandoval? *Street ball?*"

Things had gotten very quiet. The coach was waiting, half smiling. And Kenny felt stupid. But he said it. "Yes. If you want to call it that."

"Look, young man, that's not the kind of—"

"Just listen for a sec. You *asked* if we wanted to say anything."

Every breath seemed to catch. The coach looked as though someone had just knocked him over the head.

But he listened.

"I think that sometimes Miles ought to get the ball in situations where he *can* go one-on-one."

"I'll tell you what that leads to, Sandoval. It's all that dribble-behind-the-back, three-sixty spin stuff. The guys who do that care more about making fancy moves than they do about putting the ball in the basket."

"You mean *black* players, don't you?"

"*What?*"

"You're saying that's how blacks play."

"You better watch what you're saying to me, young man. This has *nothing* to do with skin color. It's the *style of play* I don't like."

"I don't know about that. But I know I can't guard Miles and stop him. I don't know anyone who can. If two guys have to cover him, then that leaves somebody open. Or if—"

"All right, Sandoval, I'll tell you what. Since you know so much about the game, you come out here and coach. You show me how all this is going to happen. I'll just plunk myself down in the bleachers and watch."

Coach Donaldson's neck was all blotched with red marks, and his voice was tight. The players could sense he was working hard to stay under control.

"Well, okay. I'm not saying I'm a coach

or anything. But I'll try to show you what I mean. Or at least Miles will."

Kenny got up and motioned for the players to come with him. They walked slowly onto the floor, but they looked doubtful.

Kenny stepped over to Miles. "You gotta help me," he said.

"No problem," Miles said.

Kenny saw the spark in Miles's eyes. He suddenly felt a lot better.

So Kenny let Miles do the coaching.

Miles had the kids run one of Coach Donaldson's plays. But he added a twist. The players set their screens, but then they rolled to the left side of the key.

Tommy got the ball at the foul line and passed to Miles. Then Tommy also cut to the left. All the players except Miles ended up on one side of the court.

"Okay, that's called 'clearing out.' Let's try it with a defense," Miles said. "Man-for-man this first time."

Kenny joined the other nonstarters on defense, and he guarded Derek. Brett was on Miles.

The players cleared out to the left side.

Miles got the ball. He had a lot of room and just one defender to face. He gave a head fake and then drove straight past Brett for a lay-up. Brett just wasn't quick enough to stay with the guy.

"All right, let's try it again," Miles said. "But defense, go all out to stop me this time. And use a zone."

Miles walked over and whispered something to Harlan.

This time the offense cleared out again. But Stephanie and Brett, on defense, both went after Miles.

Miles dribbled to the right. But Stephanie and Brett sandwiched him, and he was trapped.

So Miles went up for an off-balance jumper—not a good shot.

At that moment Harlan rolled around his defender and cut to the basket.

The shot was not a shot at all.

It was a pass.

Miles hit Harlan, who was left open in the zone—with three defenders trying to cover four players.

Bingo. Two points.

"See," Miles said, "clearing out doesn't always mean the one-on-one guy shoots. Sometimes that player draws double coverage and opens someone else for the shot."

Kenny saw that the players liked the idea. They knew what Miles could do for them. Kenny glanced at Coach Donaldson, who was watching and listening. His face was like stone.

Miles showed the players some more options. If Harlan rolled to the basket and a defender picked him up, Josh would break to the foul line for a pass.

Someone had to be open if Miles was doubled.

After that, Miles said, "One more thing. We've got some fast players, so we need to run more. We've done all right on a few fast breaks, but we don't get them started often enough."

Kenny was amazed at how much Miles was talking. And he knew what he was talking about. Anyone could see that.

Miles showed Josh and Harlan how to take the rebound, spin, and look for the outlet pass.

He had one guard release quickly for a lead pass.

The other one moved to an outlet spot, wide to one side or the other. That player would take the pass and then push the ball up the floor.

Miles showed the players how to run lanes, keep passing, and not bunch together.

Kenny could see how the fast break could help the team get the advantage on bigger players who weren't quite so quick.

And even more than that, Miles's enthusiasm was catching. Everyone was having fun and looking excited.

Miles hardly seemed to be the same guy.

Derek was yelling, "Hey, we're going to *destroy* those big, slow guys. I think I'll use my *slam dunk* shot."

For the first time all season, the players were laughing. "Yeah, do that," Miles told him. "But you'll have to carry a chair with you."

And then Kenny saw Coach Donaldson stand up and walk onto the floor. Now what?

The coach waited until the kids ran an-

other break, and then he said, "All right.
Let me talk to you. Come over here."

Everyone walked over. Kenny felt the high
spirits close down as everyone got quiet
again.

"All right, now listen," Coach Donaldson
said, and he sounded firm. "I don't dis-
agree with what Harris has been telling
you—not entirely. For one thing, I was
planning to work more on our fast break
today."

He planted his feet rather wide and folded
his arms over his chest. "I still don't like this
one-on-one business. Harris makes it sound
organized and unselfish. But that's not how
it turns out, in my experience."

He paused.

Everyone was standing stiff, waiting.

Just when Kenny expected the worst,
however, Coach Donaldson said, "But if you
kids think that's what you want to do, go
ahead and try it in the next game. Establish
your offense first, though. And Harris, don't
turn it into a hot-dog act. If you do that, I'll
shut it down."

Kenny couldn't believe it. The coach was
actually giving in.

But now he said, sternly, "All right, we've got a lot of work to do. Harris didn't show you quite *everything* there is to know about this game."

Kenny knew that was the coach's way of putting Miles down a little. But Miles looked at Kenny and smiled. They both knew they had won a victory.

That was enough for today.

Now or Never

Coach Donaldson took charge of practice from that point on. He told the forwards and centers, "Fast breaks are fine, but you can't break if you don't get the rebound. That means you've *got* to get position and block out those taller players."

And so the players worked on positioning for rebounds. And then they went back to outlet passes and running the break.

And something was starting to happen.

Kenny could feel it.

The team was playing with some fire. They were using the one advantage they would have over the bigger teams—*speed.*

Everyone was yelling back and forth,

supporting each other—laughing, cheering, slapping hands. It was great.

Coach Donaldson didn't exactly encourage any of that. But he didn't stop it either. The players were not only showing more excitement; they were putting the ball in the basket.

When practice was over, Kenny and Harlan left the building together. They were unlocking their bikes when Miles came out of the building and came over to them.

"Kenny," he said, "I can't believe you stood up to the coach that way."

"You're the one who knew what to do," Kenny said.

"Yeah. But I couldn't have gotten it started. He never would have listened to me."

"Do you still think he's prejudiced against you?"

"Sure I do."

"Why do you even want to play for him then?" Harlan asked.

"I don't. But after that one practice, I told my dad I was quitting. He said, 'No way. You go out there and *show* the man.' The only thing is, I wasn't getting a chance to show him—until now."

Kenny didn't know what to say.

Miles seemed a little embarrassed too. "Besides, we could still have a pretty good team," he finally said.

"You think so?" Harlan asked.

"I really do," Miles said. "I'll tell you what, Harlan. You're not fast, and you can't help that. But if you drive hard to the basket on offense—and get some rebounds on defense—this team can do something."

"Yeah. I have to do that."

"And Kenny," Miles said, "you could be one of the best players on the team. You have a *feel* for the game. But you've got to get in the flow. You're pressing too hard."

"I know. I have to stop letting the coach bother me so much," Kenny said.

"That's right. We both have to do that," Miles said.

"The whole team does," Harlan said.

"I think we can do it, too," Kenny said.

He was about to get on his bike when Miles said, "Well, anyway, catch you later . . . *brothers*." He grinned.

"Yeah. Later, bro," Kenny said, and he laughed.

And Harlan said, "We'll see you, Miles."

But Miles hesitated. "Back in LA, you know, most of the time I wasn't called Miles."

"What did people call you?" Harlan asked.

"Tip."

"Tip?"

"You know, from being able to make tip-in shots."

"Okay, Tip," Kenny said. "We'll see you at the next practice."

Tip nodded and smiled. Kenny had never seen him look quite so happy.

The team practiced again on Thursday. The coach had them run their plays. At times, though, when Tommy held up an open hand, the team would clear out and get the ball to Miles. Or they would clear out to the opposite side and pass to Josh.

Everything worked great against the second team. But would it work on Saturday?

The game was with the Santa Rita Jazz. A girl on the team named Jorgensen was supposed to be a great shooter. And Kenny

knew Palmer, the point guard—a good athlete.

But the Santa Rita star was a guy named
"Knees" Beesley. He was a giant—a sixth
grader almost six feet tall.

And Knees was more than just tall. He
was strong, and he had good moves close to
the basket.

When Saturday came, and the game got
started, big Beesley showed exactly what he
could do. The first two times the Jazz shot—
and missed—Beesley crashed the boards,
grabbed the rebound, and laid the ball back
in.

Coach Donaldson yelled, "Come on, Harlan, you gotta block out."

And Miles ran over and said something
to Harlan.

Kenny saw Harlan nod, and then, the next
time the Jazz came on offense, Harlan stayed
with Beesley—like glue.

When Palmer took a shot from outside,
Harlan twisted around but kept his body
right on the big guy. He braced himself, with
his legs set, and he kept his elbows spread
wide.

This time, Harlan went up for the rebound, and Beesley tried to go over him. The whistle sounded. The ref called an "over-the-back" foul on Beesley.

The next time it happened, Beesley was a little more careful.

This time, Harlan got the rebound, spun, and passed to Tommy on the sideline. Derek broke down the floor. Tommy led him with a good pass. And Derek went in for the easy lay-up.

Kenny could see that the Jazz had very little speed. The fast break would work if the Lakers could keep rebounding.

But on offense the Jazz players were feeding the ball to Beesley when they could. And he was tough to stop.

He didn't dribble well. But he could take one step and lay the ball up. In close, Josh tried to help Harlan defend the guy, but it was a battle.

The Jazz built up a 14 to 9 lead.

Coach Donaldson told the Lakers to stick with his offense for now, and not to clear out. He said they needed to show their offense and get it running before they went to other options.

But Miles was getting open—even without the offense clearing out for him. And he was hitting his jump shot.

The Jazz defense was soon keying on Miles, trying to keep him from getting the ball.

That meant Josh started to get some room to work.

He drove to the basket for an easy hoop that brought the Lakers to a 14 to 11 score.

Beesley got the two points back at the other end of the floor. But then Josh popped a jumper from "inside the paint."

And this time the Lakers defense got tough. Miles slipped in and stole a pass meant for Beesley.

Josh got the ball again and drove to the hoop. He didn't get the basket, but he drew a foul . . . *on Beesley.* That was two on him.

The Jazz coach decided to put the big guy on the bench before he picked up another one.

And that was the opening the Lakers needed.

Derek did miss a wide-open shot. But at the other end of the court, Harlan grabbed a rebound and passed quickly to Tommy.

The Lakers took off, with a three-on-two advantage.

The Jazz defended well, and didn't give up a lay-up. Tommy had to pull up for a jumper. He missed, but Miles jumped high and tipped the ball into the hoop.

"Way to go, *Tip*!" Kenny shouted from the bench.

Derek slapped hands with Miles as the two ran back down the court.

"Tip—that's a good name for you," Derek yelled.

"That *is* my name," Miles shouted back. He was beaming.

The Lakers were suddenly having fun.

Kenny heard Tommy yell, "Let's try the clear-out."

The next time they got the ball, Tommy held up an open hand. The Lakers cleared to the left of the lane. Tommy faked a pass to the post, just as Miles burst away from his defender.

Tommy fed the ball to Miles.

He caught the ball and looked his defender in the face. Jeff Packard—the guy defending Miles—was a good athlete, and pretty good-sized.

Miles gave him a couple of head fakes, but Packard held his ground. So Miles dribbled to the right and took Packard toward the corner.

Then—*bam*—he switched hands on the dribble and burst past Packard on the left.

He was heading for the hoop.

But Jorgensen broke toward him.

Bang. Miles hit Josh with a bullet pass right under the basket!

Josh laid the ball up and in.

Two points.

And the Lakers were making their move. They had the lead now, 17 to 16.

The Jazz took a time-out to talk things over.

Coach Donaldson actually sounded excited when his team came to the sideline. "All right. Now we're making it happen," he said. He was actually patting the kids on the back.

But the Jazz hadn't decided to give up and go home. They came back with a zone defense. And Beesley was back.

Beesley had to be careful not to foul. But even so, the big guy could still do a lot of damage.

The next time the Lakers cleared out, Miles beat his man and took a short jump shot. But Beesley left his man and jumped high. He blocked the shot out of bounds.

The battle was on.

Kenny and Jackie got into the game late in the half. Jackie had a better knack than Tommy for getting the ball to the open player. That added more pressure on the Jazz.

Kenny played tough defense. And he felt more confident with the ball today.

He came off a screen and got a nice pass from Jackie. He dribbled twice and pulled up for a shot. When he released the ball, he knew it was in.

The ball snapped the strings.

And Kenny felt *good*.

"That's it," Miles yelled to him. "Now you're in the flow. Keep it up."

Kenny yelled to his teammates, "All right. Let's do it. Tough defense. Let's get the ball back."

But Jorgensen knocked in a three-pointer from outside.

The Jazz were going to battle all the way.

When halftime came, the Lakers had the lead. But it was only two points, 29 to 27.

The Lakers needed a win—bad—but it wasn't going to be easy.

★ 8 ★

Now!

During halftime Coach Donaldson talked *hard*. But he didn't sound quite the same as he had the last two weeks.

"You look a lot better," he told the players. "But you're still letting down on some things. Harlan, you can't let that big guy post up so close to the basket. It's too easy for him to get lay-ups from there."

"I can't push him, Coach. He's too big," Harlan said.

"That's why you have to get down the floor first and get set. Take that spot away from him. If he tries to go through you, he'll pick up a foul. And that's just what we want."

"Coach?" Miles said.

"Yeah."

"Maybe we should drive at Knees and try to get him in foul trouble."

"Okay. Good point, Miles. I'm thinking the same thing. Let's clear out and let Miles drive straight at him. If we can get a couple of quick fouls on the guy, he'll be in big trouble."

"Don't worry. He's slow. I'll either beat him or get the foul."

"Yeah, well, let's see you *do* it before you start bragging about it."

"Okay," Miles said, and he laughed.

And the coach sort of smiled—maybe. It was a tough call. But Kenny thought the corners of his mouth moved just a little.

But then the coach really surprised Kenny. "Derek," he said, "I'm going to have Kenny start the second half. He's quicker, and someone's got to stop that point guard. Kenny, get on him tight, and stay with him."

Kenny nodded, and he tried to look confident. But his stomach was suddenly doing backflips. Finally, he was going to get a real chance to show what he could do.

Jackie patted him on the shoulder and said, "Shut Palmer down, Kenny."

Kenny felt bad for Jackie. She deserved to be playing too. She had proved it again today. When was the coach going to see that?

The team went back out for the second half. Kenny kept taking deep breaths. He didn't want to let himself get too nervous.

Up in the bleachers, Kenny heard his parents cheering him on. He knew they were excited that he had cracked the starting lineup, at least for now.

"Are you ready?" Miles asked Kenny, as they walked onto the court.

"Yeah. I think so."

"Don't worry. You can do it!" They slapped hands.

On the sidelines, Derek yelled, "Pull Palmer's shorts down around his ankles, Kenny. That'll slow him down."

Kenny didn't think he'd try that. But the first time Palmer dribbled the ball down the floor, Kenny set out to prove he could stop the guy.

He got in front of him and stayed tight. He shuffled backward, and he stayed low and ready. He faked some grabs at the ball, just to keep Palmer on his toes.

As Palmer crossed the ten-second line, he turned and got his body between Kenny and the ball. At the same time, he looked down the court and tried to spot someone open for a pass.

Finally the other guard—a little guy named Joey Myrer—came up to help. Palmer passed the ball to him.

Kenny stayed right with Palmer, close. He kept him from getting a pass back. Kenny hoped that would throw the Jazz offense off, since Myrer wasn't as good a ball handler.

All the same, Myrer got the ball to Jorgensen. And she fed the ball to Beesley.

Trouble!

But Beesley wasn't in his usual spot. Harlan had kept him from setting up as deep as he liked. Beesley tried to dribble and go to the hoop, but Harlan blocked his way.

Miles slipped in on Beesley and knocked the ball loose.

Harlan chased the ball down and hit Tommy with a quick pass.

Kenny saw the break and ran hard up the

floor. Tommy took the center lane and Miles, with his speed, caught up quickly. He took a lane on the left side.

Three on one.

Kenny was out in front of the defender.

Tommy lobbed the ball ahead, but not enough. Kenny had to slow down for the pass.

But there was Miles, breaking in from the side. Kenny hit him with a bounce pass, and the defender tried to switch off.

Miles slipped by the defender and under the basket. Then he flipped the ball back to Kenny. Kenny laid it in.

Perfect!

Miles pumped his fist, and then pointed at Kenny. "Nice shot!" he called out.

"Nice *pass*!" Kenny yelled.

But Kenny didn't have time to celebrate. He covered Palmer as soon as he took the inbounds pass. He pestered him all the way down the floor.

And then Kenny heard a whistle.

For a moment he thought the referee was calling him for hacking Palmer.

But then he turned and saw that the call

was under the basket. Big Beesley had tried to push through Harlan to take up his position. He had drawn his third foul.

And he was mad.

"He pushed *me*," he told the ref.

"No. He was set. You ran into him," the referee barked back.

Kenny heard Miles say to Tommy, "Okay, let's drive on him now. Let's get number four."

And the next time the Lakers got the ball, they did just that. Tommy called for a clear-out. He passed the ball to Miles.

Miles drove to the left, hesitated, then shot ahead again. He got a step on his defender and went right at big Beesley.

Knees stepped up and blocked his way. But Miles cut to the right and went past him.

Beesley tried to shift in front of Miles, but he was too late. He knocked the shot away, but the whistle blew.

Blocking foul on Beesley.

Beesley put up a big fuss, but the referee just told him to quiet down before he picked up a technical.

From the sidelines, Derek was yelling, "Come on, ref. Beesley's *sorry*. Give him a second chance."

The Laker fans laughed. So did some of the players on the floor. But Kenny was keeping his game face on. He still had work to do.

Beesley didn't look surprised when his coach pulled him out of the game. He galloped off to the bench and sat down.

"Great drive," Kenny told Miles.

And Kenny knew the truth. He could see that Miles did too.

This game was over.

Without their big man in the game, the Jazz didn't have much going for them.

Coach Donaldson brought in Jackie and Brett. The Lakers lost some shooting with Josh out, but they gained plenty at guard with Jackie.

And now the Lakers went on a tear.

They started clearing out more often. Miles showed the Jazz some real dazzle. He drove, took jumpers, or just as often, he passed off to open players under the basket.

Jackie canned a couple of jumpers herself.

Kenny grabbed a long rebound and fired up a quick shot.

Swish!

He was in the flow.

After a time, Beesley came back, and he got a couple of more baskets off easy rebounds. Stephanie and Ben were in the game, and they had a lot of trouble stopping him.

But Miles went to work on him again and drew the fifth foul.

From that point on the Lakers ran away with the game. The final score was 64 to 41.

And when the final buzzer sounded, the Lakers went nuts.

They had finally won a game!

More than that, Kenny was sure they would win a lot more from now on.

The coach didn't do any jumping around, but he congratulated every player. He told Kenny, "That's the best you've played. You took that point guard out of the game. And that made a big difference."

"Miles was the one who made it all happen, Coach," Kenny said.

Miles had just stepped up to slap hands with Kenny.

Coach Donaldson nodded. "Good job, Harris," he said. "You still do more hotdogging than I like, but I'll have to admit, you made the one-on-one work. You're all right."

When the coach walked away, Miles said, "It almost broke his jaw to tell me I did okay." He laughed.

"I think he's coming around," Kenny said. "He could have been really mad at us for taking over practice that day. That wasn't easy for him."

"That's not the hardest. He doesn't like to think some *street player* knows something about basketball."

But now Miles's parents were grabbing him. His mom hugged him. Then his dad grabbed him. "You were great," they were both saying.

"Kenny, good job," Mr. Harris said. "Miles told us what you did at practice the other day. That took some courage."

Kenny sort of shrugged. He saw his parents coming, and he turned to give his mom a hug.

But he could still hear Mr. Harris talking to Miles.

"Come on," he said. "Get showered. Let's go get some lunch. We'll celebrate."

Kenny was getting hugged by his own dad about then, but he heard Miles say, "Naw. That's all right. I want to ride my bike home with my friends."

Kenny looked around and smiled.

Miles gave him a high five.

League Standings After Three Games

Angel Park Bulls	2–0
Blue Springs Warriors	2–0
Santa Rita Jazz	2–1
Paseo Rockets	1–1
Angel Park Lakers	1–2
San Lorenzo Suns	1–2
Cactus Hills Clippers	0–3

First Game Scores:

Angel Park Bulls	56	Angel Park Lakers	39
San Lorenzo Suns	36	Cactus Hills Clippers	19
Santa Rita Jazz	44	Paseo Rockets	40
Blue Springs Warriors	bye		

Second Game Scores:

Blue Springs Warriors	42	Angel Park Lakers	31
Paseo Rockets	51	San Lorenzo Suns	42
Santa Rita Jazz	66	Cactus Hills Clippers	23
Angel Park Bulls	bye		

Third Game Scores:

Angel Park Lakers	64	Santa Rita Jazz	41
Angel Park Bulls	49	San Lorenzo Suns	45
Blue Springs Warriors	38	Cactus Hills Clippers	29
Paseo Rockets	bye		

Angel Park Hoop Stars Strategies

Attack from the Wing

What could beat the heart-pounding thrill of sinking a clutch 20-foot buzzer-beater? Sure, scoring is fun. But you need more than luck on a winning team. You need patience, teamwork, and strategy. Basically, the closer the shooter is to the basket, the more likely the ball is to drop. Think about it: with two seconds left would you rather take a lay-up or a jumper?

Traditionally, play begins at the **point**. Passing from point-to-post or point-to-corner, however, can be risky. A more effective strategy is for the point guard to swing the ball to either the off guard or forward playing at the **wing**. From there the ball handler can pass to the corner, pass to the post, shoot, drive to the basket, or pass back out to the point guard to begin an attack from the other wing. By running, cutting, passing, and dribbling, players use motion to off-balance a defense and set up the easy basket.

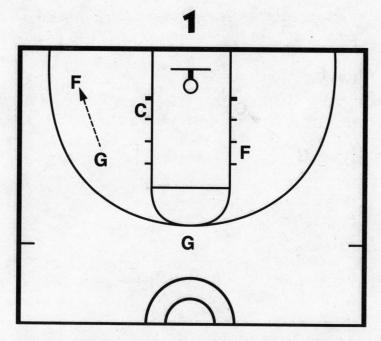

From wing position, guard may pump-fake a shot, hoping to draw defender in a step, and then make quick pass to forward in corner for easy jumper, or return pass to guard at point.

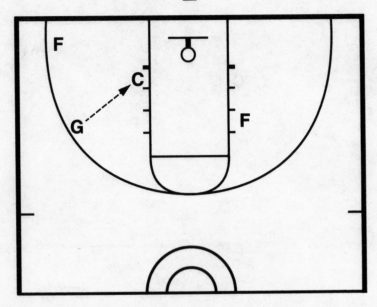

Guard makes pass to center posting low. Center may try to spin-fake defender toward hoop, or pass back to forward in corner.

3

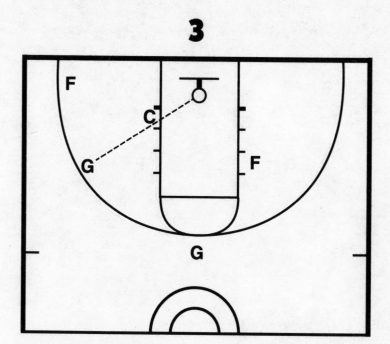

Guard takes jumper from wing position, with center and forward in post positions for rebound.

4

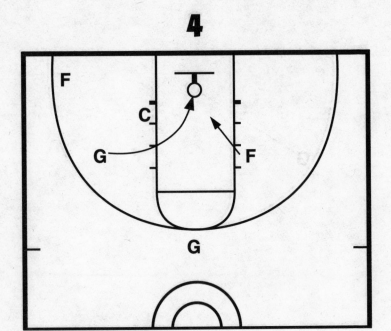

Guard drives into lane using center in low
post as a screen. Forward is in trailer position for easy rebound, pass, or tip-in.

5

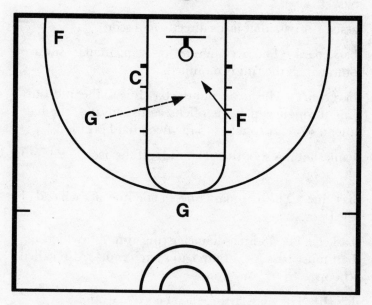

Forward posting up makes quick cut into lane for pass from guard on wing. By posting low, center is in position for easy rebound or tip-in.

Glossary

airball   An embarrassing shot that falls far short of the basket.

assist   A pass that leads directly to a score.

backboard   The rectangular or semicircular surface onto which the rim is mounted.

backcourt   The area from the baseline to the midcourt line through which the offense must advance the ball after a score. Also refers to the two guard positions.

bank shot   A shot that rebounds off the backboard into the hoop.

baseline   The boundary line, or end line, at each end of the floor.

basket   The 18-inch-diameter ring through which the ball must pass for a player to score points. Also called "hoop," "rim," or "iron."

bench   The nonstarting members of a team.

block   To repel a shot at any point on its upward arc. Also called "reject."

box out   To square the body toward the basket in an effort to screen an opponent from getting a rebound. Also called "block out."

brick   A low-arc shot that bangs clumsily off the rim. Taking terrible shots is called "throwing up bricks."

center   The middle position in a three-player front line, usually the tallest member of the team.

charge   A foul on a ball handler for running into a stationary defensive player who has established position.

clear out   To free, or isolate, a ball handler to go one-on-one with a defender by rotating offensive players to the opposite side of the floor.

crash the boards To hustle for rebounds coming off the backboard.

cut A quick move by a player without the ball toward the basket for a possible pass.

double dribble An infraction in which a ball handler dribbles with both hands simultaneously or resumes a dribble after having stopped.

double-team Two players defending one opponent, also called "trapping."

downtown A shot taken far away from the basket.

drive To dribble hard toward the basket for a close shot at the goal.

fake Any move by a ball handler to deceive a defender into an off-balance position, such as a "head fake" or "pump fake."

fast break A hustling transition offense in which players move quickly upcourt before opponents can fall back on defense.

forward Either of the two outside positions in a three-player front line.

foul Illegal contact or unsportsmanlike conduct that may result in either a change of possession or a free throw for the player fouled.

free throw An undefended shot at the basket from a distance of 15 feet from the end line, awarded to a player who has been fouled.

free throw lane The 12-foot-wide rectangular area inside the free throw lines. Also called the "lane," "underneath," or the "paint."

give and go   A maneuver in which a player passes to a teammate, cuts to the basket, and looks for a quick return pass.

guard   Either of the two backcourt positions. A point guard usually calls plays and brings the ball upcourt; the off guard is often the team's best shooter.

hail mary   A desperation shot at the basket.

held ball   When opposing players have equal possession of the ball, resulting in a "jump ball." Instead of jumping, however, most teams today alternate possession as indicated by the possession arrow.

inbound   To bring the ball into play after a score, turnover, or other stoppage of play.

jump ball   The play that begins the game wherein a ball is tossed into the air above and between two opposing players by the referee.

key   The area that includes the free throw lane and free throw circle.

man-to-man defense   A method of defense in which each member of the defensive team is designated to guard a particular member of the offensive team.

midcourt line   The boundary that divides the playing surface into two equal halves, also called the "ten-second line."

outlet pass   A transition pass from a rebounder to a teammate usually positioned at or near either sideline.

pivot   The act of keeping one foot in place while holding the ball and moving the other foot one step in any direction.

point   A position in the front court, usually at the top of the key. A point guard might "pull up" here to signal a play.

post   The position the center plays on offense. In a "high post," the center plays near the top of the free throw circle. In a "low post," the center plays near the basket.

press   An aggressive type of defense in which players guard opponents very closely, designed to induce an opponent into committing a turnover.

rainbow   A pretty outside shot with a very high arc, as opposed to an airball.

screen   An offensive play in which a teammate, by establishing position, blocks a defender from guarding the ball handler, leaving him open for an uncontested shot. Also called a "pick."

shot   An aimed throw of the ball at the hoop. Familiar shots are the "jump shot," the "lay-up," the "hook shot," the "slam dunk," the "fadeaway jumper," and the "three-point shot."

showtime   Fast-paced and flashy style of play.

switch   A maneuver in which two teammates on defense shift assignments so that each guards the opponent usually guarded by the other.

ten seconds   The amount of time an offensive team has to inbound the ball from the baseline past the midcourt—or "ten-second"—line. A violation results in change of possession.

three-seconds violation   An infraction in which an offensive player remains inside the free throw lane for more than the permitted three seconds at a time.

tip-in   A field goal made when a player taps the ball in after a missed field goal attempt.

trailer   A player who follows closely, or "trails," a ball handler driving to the basket, either to rebound or to receive a quick pass for a basket.

transition   The act of switching from defense to offense, and vice versa.

travel   An infraction in which a ball handler takes more than two steps without dribbling or passing, resulting in a turnover. Also called "walk."

turnover   The loss of possession of the ball to the opposing team, through mistakes or infractions of the rules.

wings   The areas just below the free throw line and to the sides of the lane. Often the best point to begin an offensive attack.

zone defense   A method of defense in which each member of the defensive team guards a specified portion, or "zone," of the playing area.